Penelope Pine

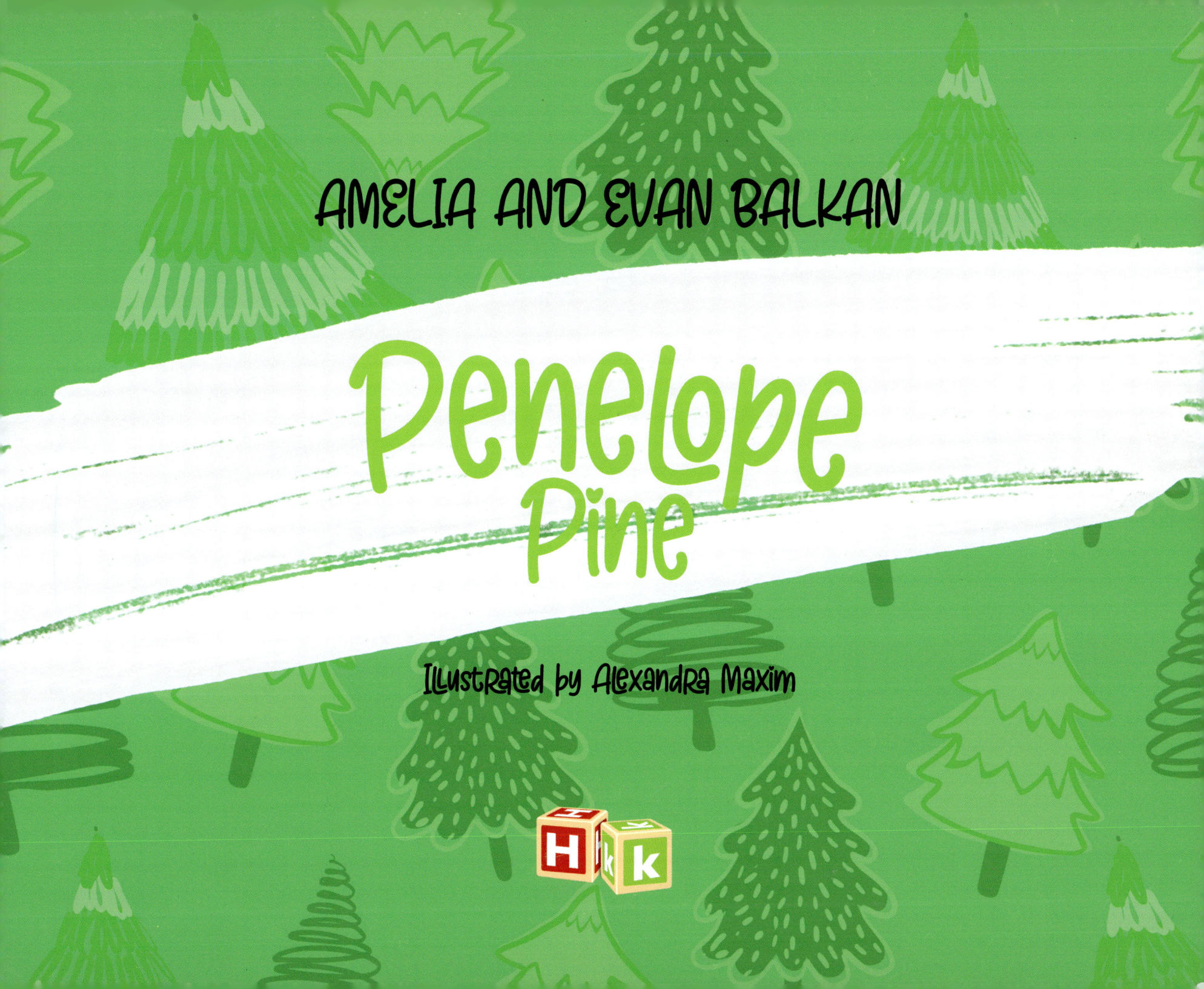

Histria Kids

Las Vegas - Oxford - Palm Beach

Published in the United States of America by
Histria Books, a division of Histria LLC
7181 N. Hualapai Way
Las Vegas, NV 89166 USA
HistriaBooks.com

Histria Kids is an imprint of Histria Books. Titles published under the imprints of Histria Books are distributed worldwide.

All rights reserved. No part of this book may be reprinted or reproduced or utilized in any form or by any electronic, mechanical or other means, now known or hereafter invented, including photocopying and recording, or in any information storage or retrieval system, without the permission in writing from the Publisher.

Library of Congress Control Number: 2020952938

ISBN 978-1-59211-086-5 (casebound)
ISBN 978-1-59211-152-7 (softbound)
ISBN 978-1-59211-233-3 (eBook)

Story Copyright © 2020 by Evan Balkan and Amelia Balkan
Illustrations Copyright © 2020 by Histria Books

Penelope was a pine tree.

No matter how hard she tried, she couldnt turn herself colors.

Penelope's friends shivered.

Penelope hadnt lost her leaves. (The truth is, she doesnt have leaves. She has needles). And so she was warm.

All the trees played together again – through the spring, and the summer, and on into autumn.

AMELIA BALKAN

Amelia Balkan, 16, is a junior at Towson High School, in Towson, Maryland. She enjoys hanging out with her dog Bella and going to the beach.

EVAN BALKAN

Evan Balkan has published seven books of nonfiction and three novels, as well as many essays and short stories. His screenplays have won numerous awards. He teaches writing at the Community College of Baltimore County and Johns Hopkins University and lives in Towson, Maryland.

Alexandra Maxim

Alexandra Maxim is an illustrator from Iasi, Romania. Born in 1993, she graduated the University of Arts in her hometown, specializing in Puppets and Marionets. She's always had a great passion for all types of art, from poetry to painting, to dancing and singing. She discovered her passion for illustrating a few years ago. Her wings are already growing big and strong.